This Walker book belongs to

....

....

....

To Adam,
     S.M^cB.

For Di,
     A.J.

First published 2007 by Walker Books Ltd
87 Vauxhall Walk, London SE11 5HJ

This edition published 2015

10 9 8 7 6 5 4 3 2 1

Text © 2007 Sam McBratney
Illustrations © 2007 Anita Jeram

Guess How Much I Love You™ is
a trademark of Walker Books Ltd, London.

The right of Sam McBratney and Anita Jeram to be
identified as author and illustrator respectively of this
work has been asserted by them in accordance with
the Copyright, Designs and Patents Act 1988.

This book has been typeset in Cochin.

Printed and bound in China.

British Library Cataloguing in
Publication Data: a catalogue record
for this book is available from the
British Library.

ISBN 978-1-4063-5743-1

www.walker.co.uk

GUESS HOW MUCH I LOVE YOU

I LOVE YOU

—— *in the* ——

SPRING

Written by

Sam McBratney

Illustrated by

Anita Jeram

WALKER BOOKS
AND SUBSIDIARIES

LONDON · BOSTON · SYDNEY · AUCKLAND

Little Nutbrown Hare
and Big Nutbrown Hare went
hopping in the spring.

Spring is when things start
growing after winter.

They saw a tiny acorn growing.

"Someday it will be a tree,"
said Big Nutbrown Hare.

"A big big tree?"

"Oh, a mighty tree,"
said Big Nutbrown
Hare.

Little Nutbrown Hare spotted a tadpole
in a pool. It was a tiny tadpole,
as wriggly as
could be.

"It will grow up to be a frog,"
said Big Nutbrown Hare.

"Like that frog over there?"

"Just the same as that one,"
said Big Nutbrown Hare.

A hairy caterpillar slowly crossed the path in front of them, in search of something green to eat.

"One day soon it will change
into a butterfly," said
Big Nutbrown Hare.

"With wings?"

"Oh, lovely wings," said
     Big Nutbrown Hare.

And then they found a bird's nest
among the rushes. It was full of eggs.

"What does an egg turn into?" asked
Little Nutbrown Hare.

"A bird."

"A big big bird?"

"Well ... a grown-up bird,"
said Big Nutbrown Hare.

Does nothing stay the same? thought Little Nutbrown Hare. Does everything change?

Then he began to laugh.

"What does a little
brown hare like
me turn into?"
he said.

Big Nutbrown Hare
began to think,

and think...

Goodness me, did he
know the answer?

Yes!

"A Big Nutbrown Hare – like me!"

Other *Guess How Much I Love You* Books

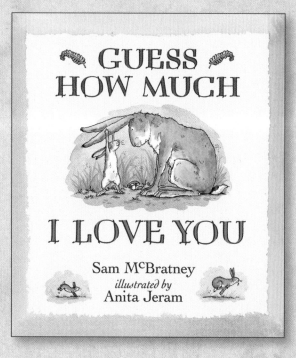